Zoe-Marie

WAIT AND SEE
A STORY ABOUT *MOVING* AND *CHANGE*

Written by Beverly Harris

Illustrated by Natasha Hamuene

ISBN: 978-1-7325911-9-6

Library of Congress Control Number: 2019915683

Contents

Dedication

This book is dedicated to military kids and to everyone who has struggled with the changes that come along in life.

Summer Fun

Zoe-Marie tucked her legs under and hit the water with a big splash. "I'll race you to the other end of the pool" she yelled to Kate who jumped into the water after her. School was closed. It was summer fun time.

For Zoe-Marie summer fun was riding her bike, taking care of her garden, and long days at the pool with friends Emma, Kate, and Matt.

Summer fun also meant camping out in the tent that Emma's dad had set up in their backyard. In the tent, they played board games, or they played games on their tablets. Other times, they went out into the yard and kicked around Zoe-Marie's soccer ball. And sometimes they played silly games that they made up about astronauts and monsters from distant galaxies.

On some nights, Zoe-Marie and her friends went out to the tent with their flashlights and sat in a circle. Then, Miss Lena, Emma's mom, would come out wearing a funny dress that had long tattered sleeves and big dark red spots on it. The spots looked like dried blood stains. She would wear a wig with fake spider webs in it, and she'd have her mouth colored bright purple with lipstick.

On those nights she would tell them what she called the "Scary Tales of Phantom Cavern". Zoe-Marie didn't think that Miss Lena's stories were all that scary. But she thought that it was fun to listen to Miss Lena, who would change her voice to a deep growl to sound like a phantom. Or sometimes roar like the two-headed leopard who according to Miss Lena, stood guard at the opening of the Phantom's Cavern to claw anyone to shreds who tried to enter.

Meet the Four Peas

Zoe-Marie's family and her friends lived on Timothy Street. Emma, Kate and Matt had lived there all of their lives. Zoe-Marie's family moved to Timothy Street when she was five. She met Emma, Kate, and Matt at the school bus stop on the first day of school. Emma had been the first to say hi to Zoe-Marie, next Matt told her hi, and then Kate. They became friends that day. Now, they were eight and still best friends. They walked to school together in the mornings, and they walked home together when school was over in the afternoon. They didn't eat lunch together because they were in different classes and everyone had to eat with the kids in their class. But the four of them played together after lunch during recess.

The four friends liked all the same foods; pepperoni pizza was their favorite. They all loved basketball and soccer, and they all agreed that "The Space Zombie" was the best movie ever made.

One day when Zoe-Marie was six, her mom looked at the group of friends. She shook her head and told them, "You all are just like four peas in a pod. You are to-gether all the time, and each one of you is like the other."

It was true they were as alike as four peas lined up in one giant pod when it came to things they liked to eat and do. But there was one big difference; peas in a pod all look alike, but the four friends did not look alike.

Zoe-Marie was a tall slender girl with large dark eyes and long black hair that curled around her shoulders. Her skin was the color of cocoa. In her school pictures, Zoe-Marie always stood in the back row with the taller kids. Standing in the back row suited her fine because she was shy and liked to stay out of the spotlight of the front row.

Zoe-Marie's friend Emma was just the opposite. She was not shy at all. She liked to talk and giggle, and she loved to be in the spotlight. She was very fair skinned with freckles and bright red hair that she wore in a ponytail most of the time. She loved animals and wanted to open a clinic to take care of sick animals someday. She had a pet rabbit named Herman and a hamster named Zorro.

Matt wasn't shy either, he liked to tell funny jokes that made his friends crack-up with laughter.

He was the only boy that lived on their street. He was a little shorter than Zoe-Marie but still pretty tall. Matt's skin was dark brown, he had thick curly brown hair and he wore eyeglasses.

Zoe-Marie could tell that Matt wished other boys lived on their street. Last year when he found out that he was going to get a new little brother or sister, he was very excited! He told his friends, "I hope that I get a little brother, that would be great! Then there'd finally be another boy on this street". But he got a little sister instead. Her name was Ivy; Zoe-Marie thought she was cute.

Kate had dark eyes that sparkled when she smiled. Her black hair was cut into a short bob. She was a quiet girl who liked to paint and draw. Zoe-Marie, Matt, and Emma all had their birthdays in the winter or spring. They could invite their other friends from school to their parties. But Kate was a few months younger than the rest of them. Her birthday wasn't until July. In July most of their school friends were away on vacation. That meant there was no one from school to come to Kate's birthday celebrations. So, Zoe-Marie, Matt, and Emma were usually Kate's only party guests.

All of Kate's parties were fun, but this year her party had been awesome. It was held at a big arcade center. The arcade center had dozens of fun games, a go-kart track, and three bounce houses. Kate, Zoe-Marie, Matt, and Emma were given forty game tokens, enough to play twenty games. They had a big pepperoni pizza to eat. When the party was over Kate's mom handed everyone a gift bag that was filled with all kinds of toys and treats for them to take home.

A Change is Coming

Zoe-Marie wanted her summer fun to go on forever. But she knew that it wouldn't. And she knew at the end of summer vacation, she and her parents were going to move away.

They were moving because Zoe-Marie's mother was getting a new job. Her mother was a soldier. She was in the Army. Zoe-Marie was proud that her mom was a soldier. She knew the job that she did, helped to keep everyone safe.

Sometimes, work took her away from home for weeks or months. When her mother was away, Zoe-Marie thought having a mom that was a soldier was hard. Now, Mom was getting a new job. This new job meant that Zoe-Marie's family had to move away from her friends, her pool, and all the things that she liked to do.

Mom told Zoe-Marie about the move one hot day last June. Zoe-Marie had just come home from school, when mom said to her, "I have a surprise for you."

"What is it?" Zoe-Marie had asked, hoping that the surprise was a trip to get ice cream. Mom answered her, "We are going to move to Italy." "Move to Italy?" A very surprised Zoe-Marie asked. "That's right," her mom told her. Mom had been smiling, but Zoe-Marie hadn't felt like smiling at all. Then Mom said to Zoe-Marie, "It will be fun to live in Italy. Look at the pictures in this book, we can visit all of these places." Mom turned the pages and held the book so that Zoe-Marie could see the pictures.

Zoe-Marie thought it would be nice to visit Italy, but not to move there. She explained to her mom "I don't want to move, Emma, Kate, and Matt all live here. This is our home." Her mom told her "Zoe-Marie, you will get new friends and a new home. Besides, you can still be friends with Emma, Kate, and Matt. You don't have to stop being their friend because we move away."

Zoe-Marie felt sad when she thought about the move. As tears rolled down her cheeks that day, she had told her mother, "It won't be the same, I will have to go to a new school. What if the kids don't like me? I won't have any friends. And I won't know my way around a new school, either. What if I get lost trying to find my classroom?"

She was about to tell her mom again that she didn't want to move when mom said gently, "Zoe-Marie, we have to move. I wish I didn't have to take you away from your friends and your school. You know I'm a soldier. It is my job to serve our country. I don't have a choice about the move. But you don't have to worry. I promise you that dad and I will try our best to make our move easy and fun for you. Everything will work out fine; just wait and see."

Then her mom had bent down and hugged her, and told her, "Don't worry about the kids at the new school. A lot of them will be new there too because their parents are in the Army like me. They won't know anyone either. But I bet that they will be happy to have you for a new friend. You can use SKYPE to talk to Matt, Emma, and Kate. It will almost be the same as being here with them. Italy will be a great adventure and remember you still get to spend this summer with your friends. You can be the four peas in a pod for the whole summer." Mom had smiled down at Zoe-Marie again and said, "Now dry your eyes, and let's look at some more of these pictures of Italy."

That day after the talk with mom, Zoe-Marie had tried to put the move out of her mind. She went on with school, and when school closed, she thought about the pool, her garden, and her friends as if nothing was going to change. She didn't talk to mom or dad about the move, and she barely said anything about it to her friends. She secretly hoped her family would not need to move at all.

Moving Day

Skye was Zoe-Marie's dog and her other best friend. She was a small furry brown dog with a long body, short legs, and long floppy ears. Skye liked to run and to bark. She followed Zoe-Marie everywhere, and she slept on Zoe-Marie's bed at night.

Sock tug was Skye's favorite game. To play sock tug, Zoe-Marie would dangle an old sock and Skye would grab it with her teeth and pull it hard. She would try to get the sock away from Zoe-Marie. Skye would tug on the sock until Zoe-Marie let go of it and let her win the game. Then Skye would run to the far end of the room with the sock in her mouth. She would prance around for a few moments and then run back to Zoe-Marie as fast as she could to begin another game.

One morning near the end of summer, Zoe-Marie and Skye were in her bedroom playing sock tug. They stopped playing when they heard the rumble of what sounded like a truck engine outside. Zoe-Marie ran to the window, looked out, and saw that a truck had pulled up in front of her house. The truck was a blue-purple color. It had the words 'MOVING COMPANY' painted along its side in big red letters. Zoe-Marie frowned and wondered if it was the truck that was going to take all their things to their new home in Italy.

Zoe-Marie heard dad call to her from downstairs. "Zoe-Marie, come down here, please. The movers are here."

Zoe-Marie walked slowly down the stairs and stopped on the last step. She saw her dad and two men dressed in blue uniforms standing near the front door.

"Zoe-Marie, meet Jeff and Carlos," her dad told her. "They are here to pack up all our things, load them into their truck and send them to our new house in Italy."

"Hello there, Zoe-Marie," the man that dad had called Carlos said to her with a big smile. "We will be in your room to pack everything later today."

Zoe-Marie tried to be polite but didn't feel like talking. She didn't answer Carlos. Instead, she sat down on the step with Skye.

"Zoe-Marie does not want to move," dad told Carlos and Jeff.

Jeff, the other mover, took a big roll of brown tape from his bag and pulled a long piece off the roll. Before he bent over to pick up a cardboard box to put the tape on, he paused a moment and said to Zoe-Marie, "I visited Italy once. I really liked it. There are a lot of interesting things to see and the pizza in Italy is really good.

Zoe-Marie thought, I want to stay here in my home and eat pizza with my friends.

Zoe-Marie's dad could tell that she did not want to talk. When the moving men went into the other room, dad said in a squeaky voice, "Zoe, Zoe, Zoe your toes are showy," and then he made a funny face at her. Zoe-Marie couldn't help but giggle. Dad always did funny things to cheer her up when she was sad. Then he made his voice sound funny like he was under water. He made his lips look like a fish and said, "You and Skye come on into the kitchen with me. I am hungry for a grilled cheese sandwich, and I need your help. You know I am an awful cook, just awful."

Zoe-Marie giggled again; she knew her dad was only teasing about needing her help. He was a good cook. And his grilled cheese sandwiches were Zoe-Marie's favorite lunch.

Lunch Time

Zoe-Marie and Skye followed Dad into the kitchen. "You get the bread and cheese for the sandwiches, Zoe-Marie," he said, while he looked into the pantry for his favorite pan.

"May I get some vegetables from my garden to make us a salad?" Zoe-Marie asked her dad.

"Good idea," he told her. He went on, "But before you head outside, let's talk. When you came downstairs to meet the movers, why did you have such a long face?"

Zoe-Marie began to explain, "Everything is perfect here where we live now, Dad. I like my friends, my school, and my room. I don't want to move away."

Dad looked thoughtful for a moment and told Zoe-Marie, "Your mom and I like it here too, and Italy will be new for all of us. I think that living there is going to be super fun. Mom has to move, and we are lucky because we can go with her. Sometimes when soldiers move their families can't go with them. But you don't have to worry; we are always here for you to make sure things are okay. And you can always tell me and mom how you feel. After all, we are the Prescott's and we always take care of each other, right?"

Zoe-Marie looked at her dad, nodded her head, and said, "Right." But on the inside, she still wanted to keep things the way they were.

"Well, alright then," he told her. "Now that we've settled that, you can go outside and pick some vegetables. We'll make a huge, gigantic, towering monster salad," he said, laughing. Zoe-Marie grinned and headed out to the garden.

This year Zoe-Marie had her first vegetable garden. Early last March, before anyone knew about the move, Zoe-Marie had asked her parents if she could plant a garden. She had thought that it would be fun to grow some of her favorite vegetables.

Mom and dad had thought the vegetable garden was a good idea. They told Zoe-Marie they would help plant it. But it would be her job to take care of the garden after it was planted.

Then they took Zoe-Marie to a farm out in the country that sold plants and garden supplies. The farm had all kinds of tiny vegetable plants.

Mom had asked Zoe-Marie, "What kind of vegetables do you want to grow in your garden?"

Zoe-Marie thought for a minute and then told her, "I'd like to grow carrots and tomatoes. They are my favorites."

"Those are good choices," her mom had said.

"How about growing some cucumbers and lettuce too?" her dad asked. "Those are my favorites."

"Sounds good to me," Zoe-Marie answered.

Mom walked over to the end of the plant display. She motioned for Zoe-Marie and her dad to come over to where she was standing. "Look at these pepper plants.

I used to grow this kind when I was a kid on my parents' farm. Let's get some of these too, Zoe-Marie." By the time they finished with plant shopping, their cart was very full.

When they were back at home and ready to plant the garden, dad rented what he called a tiller from the hardware store. The tiller looked like a lawnmower with big sharp metal teeth. It broke up the ground in the sunny part of the backyard, where Zoe-Marie was going to plant her garden.

After Dad finished with the tiller, the ground was soft. Then the three of them started the planting. Dad and Zoe-Marie made small holes in the ground in straight lines.

Then Mom dropped a tiny plant into each of the holes. When all the plants were in the ground, Zoe-Marie gently pushed the soil back around them. Then she turned on the water hose to give each plant some water.

She took good care of the plants. She made sure each plant got lots of water every day. Grandma had told Zoe-Marie once, that plants grow better when you talk to them. So, Zoe-Marie talked to her plants every day, and they grew and grew.

Now her vegetables were big, and Zoe-Marie was out in the garden to pick some for lunch. She stooped and picked cucumbers, tomatoes, lettuce, carrots, and peppers and put them into a large basket.

She took the vegetables into the house and sat them on the kitchen table. Dad lifted the vegetables from the basket and put them into the sink to wash. "Nice job, Zoe-Marie, these vegetables look good. Now go and wash your hands. Lunch will be ready in a minute" dad told her.

Zoe-Marie washed her hands and slowly walked back to the kitchen. She had just thought of something else she would have to leave behind in the move. She would be leaving her garden. She asked, "Dad, what will happen to all the vegetables in the garden after we move?"

"Hmm," he sighed, "I don't know, Zoe-Marie. We move in a couple of days. We can't eat them all, and we can't take them with us. What do you think about having a garden party?" her dad asked with a smile and a wink of his eye.

"A garden party?" Zoe-Marie asked and perked up. She was not sure what a garden party was, but it sounded like it could be fun.

Her dad explained, "We could invite our friends over and have a vegetable picking party in your garden."

"Can we invite Emma, Kate, and Matt?" Zoe-Marie asked. Dad said, "You bet that you can invite them."

Zoe-Marie smiled, leaped out of her chair, and headed for the door. She wanted to go and tell her friends the news.

"Zoe-Marie, wait, we have not eaten our lunch yet."

"Oh yeah," Zoe-Marie laughed, "I almost forgot."

Zoe-Marie quickly munched her salad and sandwich while Skye sat near and closely watched her eat. Skye was good at getting treats. She would stand on her hind legs to beg. She often ended up with bits of cheese or chicken from Zoe-Marie and her parents.

When Zoe-Marie looked down at Skye today, the little dog sat up on her hind legs. Zoe-Marie broke off a small piece of sandwich and tossed it to Skye, who gobbled it down and wagged her tail in thanks to Zoe-Marie for the treat.

"I'm finished with my lunch, Dad. May I go outside now?" Zoe-Marie asked.

"Yes, you can go," he told her while he cleared the dishes off the table. "Have fun and remember, invite the neighbors. Tell them the party is tomorrow evening."

"Okay, Dad. I will!" Zoe-Marie yelled over her shoulder as she headed outside.

Zoe-Marie ran like a flash through the living room and down the front steps. When her feet touched the sidewalk in front of her house, she noticed little Skye at her side. She told Skye, "Let's head to Emma's house first." The little dog took off in a trot toward Emma's house.

When Zoe-Marie and Skye arrived at Emma's house, they saw her sitting on her front porch reading.

When Emma looked up from her book and saw Zoe-Marie and Skye, she smiled and ran to meet them.

"Hi, Zoe-Marie, what are you doing here?" she asked and stooped to pet Skye, who covered Emma's hand with warm licks.

Zoe-Marie told Emma all about her party plans.

Emma giggled; she thought a vegetable picking party would be awesome. "I will go with you to invite everyone else," she told Zoe-Marie.

The two girls headed off with Skye leading the way. They told Kate next and then Matt. Both of them went with Zoe-Marie and Emma to tell the rest of the neighbors on the street about the party. Zoe-Marie had such a good time inviting everyone to the garden party; that she almost forgot about the move.

Back at Home

When she arrived back home, she saw that the big moving truck was still in her driveway. She walked past the truck, up the porch steps, and into the house. The room was full of boxes. Dad was talking with the movers. He stopped when she came into the room and said, "Hi, Zoe-Marie. Did you invite everyone?"

"Yes, Dad," Zoe-Marie mumbled as she headed up-stairs to her room. In her room, she was glad to see that her bed was still in its place. But the rest of her things, except for a few pieces of clothing and her swimsuit were gone. Zoe-Marie sighed, moving is hard and unfair," she thought to herself.

She fell asleep and woke up when she heard some-one calling her name and looked up to see her mother sitting on the bed beside her. "Hi, Mom. Are the movers gone?" Zoe-Marie asked in a sleepy voice.

"They left a few minutes ago," her mom answered. "And how are you doing, little Miss Zoe-Marie?"

"I'm okay, Mom," Zoe-Marie told her. "I was thinking about the move."

"Are you still feeling a little sad about it?" her mom asked.

Zoe-Marie answered quietly, "Yes, a little."

"Zoe-Marie, it is okay to be sad. And we can talk about your feelings anytime that you need too. Now I'm going to tell you something and I want you to really think about it. It just might make you feel better about the move."

"What is it mom, Zoe-Marie asked?"

Mom began, "Life will be full of changes Zoe-Marie; moving is only one kind of change. Think about the butterflies that you studied last year at school. They began as tiny eggs. The eggs became caterpillars, they spent time in cocoons which must have been boring, and then they finally changed into butterflies. They had beautiful wings and could fly all around, exploring new places. Like those butterflies, Zoe-Marie, we must change too. We grow; we don't change into a caterpillar or grow wings, but our bodies' change and the world around us changes. There are all kinds of interesting places to see and things for us to learn about. There are lots of new friends waiting to meet you. But friends will come, and friends will go.

It's all a part of life.   Even the new friends that you meet when we move this time may not stay with you because things change. You will grow older and become a young woman. And one day, my dear Zoe-Marie, you may even meet someone that you will want to travel through life with and have a family of your own," mom told her.

"A family of my own, I'm not ready for that yet," Zoe-Marie frowned.

"I guess I am getting a little carried away," her mom said with a grin. She and Zoe-Marie both laughed.

Mom said, "I know you don't want to leave your friends, but you will never forget all the fun times that you've had with them. Things change in life, and sometimes those changes are not good. We don't get to choose, and we have to live with the change, like when your grandpa passed away last year. But sometimes we get to choose if it is a good change or a bad change."

"Mom, how can I choose if a change will be bad or good?" Zoe-Marie asked.

"You choose to make it a bad move by thinking and acting like it will be bad without even waiting to see our new home or meeting any of the people that live there. If you decide something is bad before you give it a try, you will be sad. And you may miss some fun things. Zoe-Marie, will you give this move a chance?"

Zoe-Marie sighed, "Okay, Mom, I will give it a chance. I will wait and see." Zoe-Marie knew that it would be hard, but she also knew that her mom was right.

"Awesome, now come on downstairs. I brought home burgers for dinner."

Zoe-Marie told her mom all about the garden party over dinner that night. Mom liked the plan. She thought that the garden party was a good way to share the vegetables and to say good-bye to their neighbors.

Zoe-Marie could hardly sleep when she went to bed that night. Her mind was racing with thoughts about the party. The next morning, the bright sun streamed in from the window and woke Zoe-Marie early.

"This is garden party day," Zoe-Marie thought as she hopped out of bed. She dressed quickly and hurried downstairs and into the kitchen. She knew that her mother would be down there making breakfast and that her dad would be out running like he did every morning.

"Good morning, Zoe-Marie. I'm making your breakfast. It's fruit and cereal; that's all we have left to eat. The movers packed everything else yesterday, and they will be here in a little while to get the rest of our things loaded onto the truck. They'll take our beds today too. Tonight, we'll sleep in the sleeping bags I borrowed from Miss Lena. Our plane leaves early tomorrow morning. We'll leave the sleeping bags out on Emma's porch so that we don't wake them up when we leave. Now, here's your breakfast." Mom sat the bowl on the table in front of Zoe-Marie.

"Thanks Mom," Zoe-Marie told her mother. She picked up her spoon and ate a little of the cereal from the bowl and then she put the spoon down. She told her mother, "I can't eat; I'm ready for the garden party."

Mom laughed and replied, "Zoe-Marie, the party is not until late this evening. How would you like to spend one last day at the pool? Dad is going to stay at home with the movers. So, I think us girls should take the day off, what do you think about that?"

"Yes, yes, yes, a whole day at the pool!" Zoe-Marie squealed. "Can my friends come with us?"

"I thought that you would ask that. Yes, they can come along too. I've already asked their parents. We will stop at their houses to pick them up on our way to the pool," her mom told her.

"Yay!" Zoe-Marie shouted. "This is going to be so much fun!"

Pool Day Fun

The day at the pool was great. Zoe-Marie and her friends played water paddleball and water basketball. When they got tired of those games, they took turns chasing each other with Matt's water bog. A toy that squirted water at anyone who was not quick enough to get out of its path. At noon, dad surprised them with lunch. He brought them sandwiches, cold milk, and peaches.

After they had eaten their fill, they decided to go back into the pool and relax on the water floats. They played a few games of floating ring toss. Between their games, they talked about the next school year and Zoe-Marie's move. Zoe-Marie told them what her mom had said about waiting until we get there to see if she liked her new home. "I told mom that I would wait and see, but now I am not so sure."

Kate told her, "I think your mom was right, Zoe-Marie. My cousin moved away last year. He didn't want to move, either. But now he likes his new school a lot. It has a big gym and an indoor pool. And when I visited him, I met all his new friends. They were cool, and I can see him and talk to him on SKYPE and Facetime. We can do that too so you can see us."

Emma and Matt both nodded their heads to agree with Kate. "I know we can still see each other, but it won't be the same," Zoe-Marie told them.

Matt said, "I wish that I was moving to Italy like you. I think it will be fun to live in a different country. You will get to see all sorts of things that the rest of us will only see pictures of. Can I come to visit you?"

"Me too?" Kate and Emma chimed in.

"Sure, you can," Zoe-Marie told them. She was starting to feel better about her move. She could still see Emma, Kate, and Matt. And she might even like the new kids and the new school.

With a big smile on her face, Zoe-Marie jumped off her float and back into the pool and yelled, "Last one in the water is a slimy frog!"

The pool day went by quickly for the four friends. Before they knew it, the day was over. "Come on guys, get your things together. It is time to head home," Zoe-Marie's mom called to them. She walked the happy group slowly back to their houses.

"See you at my house in a little while," Zoe-Marie told them when she waved goodbye to each of them at their door.

Mom asked her after they dropped everyone off, "Did you have a good time today Zoe-Marie?"

"I sure did, it was so much fun," Zoe-Marie told her. "And my friends think the move won't be so bad. They want to come and visit us."

"Well, Zoe-Marie, it looks like you are beginning to give our move a chance. I knew that you could do it. I am proud of you. Now run upstairs and change your clothes. Our neighbors will be here in a little while," her mom told her.

The Garden Party

The garden party was fun for everyone. Emma, Kate, Matt, Ms. Lena, little Ivy and all Zoe-Marie's neighbors were there. The neighbors brought food and music with them. Mr. Reynolds set up a grill in the backyard and cooked hamburgers and hotdogs. Mrs. Martin brought along some corn on the cob. Matt's mother brought over some strawberries. The neighbors picked all the vegetables and packed them up to carry home.

Zoe-Marie and her friends ate the food and picked a few vegetables too. But they mostly sat quietly on the front porch. They knew this was the last time they would visit Zoe-Marie at this house. This was the first time that none of the friends could think of anything to say.

It began to grow dark outside; the other party guests had gone home already. But Zoe-Marie and her friends still set together on the porch. When her mom and dad stepped out there, they were surprised to see them all still sitting there.

Mom and Dad both chuckled, "Come on, it's time for a group hug, and then I'll walk you all home," her dad told them.

The four of them hugged and said teary goodbyes. They said they would be friends forever and Zoe-Marie waved while dad marched the others down the driveway.

The Butterfly

As Zoe-Marie stood watching her friends leave, Mom handed her a gift-wrapped box. "What's this?" Zoe-Marie asked.

"Open it and take a look," her mother said in an odd voice. Zoe-Marie could see the slightest hint of a smile in the corner of Mom's mouth.

She slowly tore the wrapping off the box, under fluffy, brightly colored paper, Zoe-Marie saw an even smaller box. She opened the little box and pulled out a beautiful glass butterfly on a silver chain.

"It's a butterfly," Zoe-Marie said flatly. She held the necklace up in the light of the porch lamp to get a better look at it. "It's pretty, Mom, thanks," Zoe-Marie told her mother. She liked the necklace but was upset at the sight of seeing her friends leave and now not at all sure she wanted to move.

"Zoe-Marie, would you like to put your necklace on?" her mom asked.

"Not right now," Zoe-Marie told her, "I think I'll go to my room."

"Zoe-Marie, look at the butterfly's wings," her mom said to her. "They are open wide. This butterfly is ready to fly around and learn about the world that it lives in. It is getting ready for an adventure like you are."

Zoe-Marie looked down at her necklace again. This time, she gently touched the butterfly's wings with her finger. She thought about the things that mom, dad, and her friends had said about the move, and she smiled. She finally understood what they meant. She thought, I'll wait and see because this move could be fine; in fact, it will probably be fun.

Then she began to plan all the things that she was going to do when she moved. She thought, I will meet new kids; I will Skype with my old friends and let them meet my new friends. Plus, I will get to see all those awesome places that mom showed me in the travel books, that will be cool. I might even plant another garden, and when we leave Italy, we can have another garden party for our friends there. "Yes!" she shouted.

"Zoe-Marie, were you going to tell me something?" mom asked.

Zoe-Marie looked at her mother and said, "Mom, would you please help me put my necklace on? I want to wear it tonight."

"Oh, so you do like the necklace?" her mother asked as she fastened it around Zoe-Marie's neck.

"Yes, I really do like it," Zoe-Marie told her. "I am ready for my new adventure, just like the butterfly."

"Well," mom said with a smile, "I am glad you are ready for your new adventure because we leave for Italy first thing tomorrow morning. Now, off to sleep with you, Miss Butterfly and sweet dreams."

Zoe-Marie hugged her mom and told her goodnight; then she quickly climbed the stairs. At last, she was ready for her move.

THE END

Lightning Source UK Ltd.
Milton Keynes UK
UKHW021136080620
364519UK00004B/217